Stout

by Drayton Alan

The Quest for Beer Near Perfection

A drunkity dwarf
He drank a draft
Of drinkity drink, he drank
And every time
He'd drink a drop
Of drinkity draft, he drunk

Acknowledgments

Thank you to my family, friends, and readers.

Please enjoy!

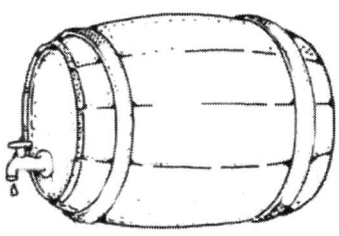

The Quest for Beer Near Perfection.

This is the story of a little person who lived large. He centered his life on searching for, and sampling, the best beers ever made. His name was Del Breowan, and even though he stood a mere three foot ten, he is remembered as a giant in the history of beer. Del faced the same challenges that any average height man does, at least any man that lives his life in pursuit of perfection.

Most of his results Del recorded and published in his newsletter, *The Brewmaster's Quarterly Gazette*. In its day, it was popular and widely read by beer artisans throughout the world. Over the years that followed his newsletter quickly became the de facto standard reference for all things brewed. It was later published in one volume, reprinted numerous times and eventually translated into German, Spanish, and Dutch. Its use as a reference lasted for many centuries after he wrote it. The original *Gazette's* information came from Del's initial work during pre-colonial times. His was an age when the blossoming knowledge of the renaissance had begun to illuminate the darkness of the Middle Ages. His work's reputation and popularity never faded, and as sometimes happened to a bellwether reference work, its reputation continued to grow over the centuries until it became the archetypal bible of beer enthusiasts everywhere. Thus, Mr. Breowan became affectionately known as the Father of Beer.

In recent years, the popularity of craft brewing has led to the humble *Brewmaster's Quarterly Gazette's Compendium* gaining a renewed interest. We are some of Mr. Breowan's most ardent admirers, and call ourselves the Beer Conservators. So, when we discovered this particular story, which was never published, we felt it our duty to do so. It was sent along with a letter to a 15th century bard known only as Anklesneeze. Anklesneeze's papers were preserved by a young nobleman, an ancestor of Lord Quimby, and found in his library at Canterhead.

We have published it here as an addition to *The Brewmaster's Quarterly Gazette Compendium*. We have added brief insights and commentary, but endeavored to present this story as originally written. The added commentary will appear in italics where we felt necessary. We hope they will be helpful to the reader.

So join with us as we consider the first new *Brewmaster's Quarterly Gazette* edition in nearly five hundred years.

The Beer Conservators

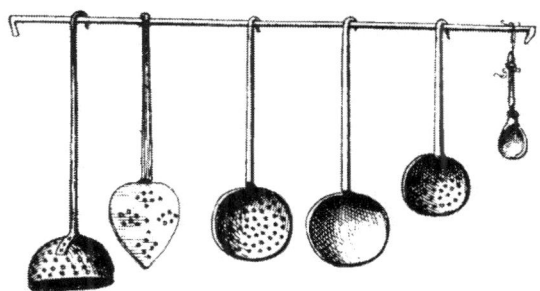

Mr. Breowan's Introduction

Conservator's Note: We have included the original introduction Del wrote in his letters here to allow the new reader to gain familiarity with Mr. Breowan's work.

My professional name is Del Breowan, Del being short for Delicious. I chose this name over my given name, Albert, since it is my life's quest to seek, describe, and share my love for tasty beer. I should mention at the outset that my passion and mode of life is that of a master brewer of beers and ales. I am a connoisseur in pursuit of beer perfection. Although I enjoy the various brews, I never drink to the point of intoxication as this would dull my ability to distinguish taste. It has been my endeavor to create the first guidebook to the various brews, which the public houses and porterhouses offer in the kingdom and beyond.

The narratives that accompany each beer are the story of my encounters and discoveries of these marvelous brews. I have included such hoping to make my work more than just a tedious book of beer-making methods and recipes. By telling the stories and the legends behind the beers I describe, I strive to give the flavor of the people and culture that produced the beer. That way the drinker might fully appreciate nuances of flavor they might otherwise have overlooked. In addition, I also tell of my personal experiences related to the discovery of such brews so that the reader may discern if such has influenced my description.

Before I begin, it is necessary for me to describe my stature, since people's reactions will, at times, color the story. I am of the people commonly referred to as 'dwarves', and events in the story might seem odd if you didn't know this. The belief that so-called dwarves, are of a race different from that of average height men, is a common misconception and wrong. I am the son of average height people and my stout stature is merely an extreme among the varieties that God has in his wisdom put among all mankind. I do not feel cheated by my lot in life, instead I embrace it, along with the challenges and rewards it offers. I am most fortunate of my kind since I have little of the twisted bones and infirmities that oft accompany such shortness. Thus, I invite you to take a view of the world from a different perspective, view of what lies beneath. Things that others may have overlooked.

Before I go any further, I would be remiss if I did not also introduce to you my young companion, Kipp Lambert. Kipp is an artist of unusual ability. He is the official illustrator of my discoveries and adventures. I've enjoyed watching Kipp create his drawings on our journeys and I am fascinated how he carefully sketches even the most mundane discovery. He can depict the various strains of barley, hops, and other ingredients in the finest detail. He also has cataloged leaf and root as well as head and grain of each plant. He has drawn much of the wonderful architecture and the unique brewing apparatuses we have seen. In addition, he's made a diligent record of several of the comely serving maids we've met along the way.

I should also mention that, although young Kipp is a veritable wizard with chalk and ink, he sometime lacks a sense of propriety. This, at times, leads to trouble when his tongue precedes his good sense. I have endeavored to school him in gentlemanly manners and tact, yet he seems a slow learner. I fear it may cause us grief if he continues his habit of speaking at the wrong time.

This time in which we live is one of knights and lords, of ignorance and of myth, where good stories are granted as much credence as truth. People are in general God-fearing and righteous. Although there are some who heed not the preaching of the friars, and lead the lives of miscreants and thieves. However, I will not glorify their waywardness nor will I encourage those evildoers by praising their acts of villainy. Yet I do relate these to give understanding to the reader and hope that such shall act as restraint upon a wayward heart.

I cannot forget to mention my appreciation for the correspondence I have received from some of you and the great insights I have gained from your letters. Thank you so much! I hope you will enjoy my *Brewmaster's Gazette* and pass it along to your friends.

Del Breowan Brewmaster

Brewmaster's Gazette: The Tale of Pallie Ale

Conservator's Note: This story is one that Del wrote intending to include as an article but had second thoughts. He decided not to publish it in the Gazette *out of respect (and fear) of upsetting the holy order of knights mentioned therein. He did however send it to Anklesneeze and made him promise not to share it until after his death. I'm certain you will enjoy the new account as much as we did.*

In this the issue of the *Brewmaster's Gazette* I shall tell a story of two beers of note, which I have featured herein. It also tells the story of how I was privileged to imbibe so rare a brew that I risk much in even telling of it.

It was a pleasant day in August when Kipp and I discovered, somewhat by accident, an anecdote so interesting we had to stop and track it down. Our chance meeting with a bard who goes by the unusual name of Anklesneeze, gave us our first clue about the so-named Paladin Ale. We are indebted to Anklesneeze, because ever afterward our retelling of his stories and songs, gained us more than one free drink for our trouble.

It started as we sat in the great room of the Drinkity Drunken Dwarf Inn. We'd been told by a passing merchant that this inn was a good place for a bed and a brew. So despite the name and its implications for my stature, we took a detour north from our route home, to lodge a night or two there and discover what we might.

I should mention that Kipp and I were coming back from a trip far to the east where I'd had an opportunity to research a new strain of hops developed near the city of Mallowhedge by some secretive monks. Kipp had assured me he would be on his best behavior during this trip and aside from the one poorly timed comment when we met the Abbot there, he'd been true to his word. The Abbot overlooked the lad's outburst; the man had the patience of a saint and the forgiveness of a martyr. Thus saving us from leaving the abbey in disrepute.

Yet, the trip's results had been a bit dubious, the "new strain" of hops were in fact ordinary hops much the same as everyone else uses. The grain, however, had been specially marinated in some method or manner the monks refused to reveal. It did have a unique flavor, but I decided not to include it in my journal. The beer is not widely available and since I had no story to share, it seemed worthless to relate. As we left, an old monk took me aside and revealed the secret in a crazy story. He said they allowed sheep to eat the grains and then induced them to regurgitate them. He claimed this softened the hulls and jumpstarted the fermentation process. Well to say the least, I didn't wait around, in case his madness was the catching sort.

The trip wasn't a total loss, since while I was in the area I successfully contacted a local brewer with extensive experience. I learned several new tricks from him. One such tip was information about a cold brewing method, which utilized a freezing process. This produced a strongly spirited beer of a most powerful nature. I took extensive notes since I was planning to attempt this on a batch of my winter harvest grains. But all of that is for another time, I have wandered far from my story.

So there we were in the Drinkity Drunken Dwarf Inn's great room, as I had mentioned. It was a wooden building with a large common room spread with tables and chairs and a long bar along the back wall. It smelled of countless pipes, spilled beer, and the pickled delicacies that lined the shelf beside the bar. A pot of something that resembled old stew and burned lentils bubbled on the hearth but no one in the place seemed brave enough to partake. A second floor was visible beyond a railing above, which surrounded the upper level of the common area.

The interior was dimly lit save a few spots of daylight that filtered in from the two windows high on the south wall. The thick smoke from pipe weed and wood fire made the light's journey from window to floor a perilous one. Little of it reached us sitting upon the oaken plank benches. The servers weren't busy; they stood around the bar. Several tables were occupied with the usual daytime denizens of such alehouses. An old bard slept face in his arms, a worn out lute leaned carelessly beside him.

I caused a stir when I walked in—I always do. I doubt the Drinkity Drunken Dwarf Inn gets many actual little people as customers. It is rare, and thus notable, for most average height people to see a man of my size. They often stare, not usually meaning to be rude, but I have grown accustomed to the reaction since it is nearly universal. To their credit, most of the patrons in the inn returned to their drinking and talking after only a moment. We found a table and after looking at a menu gave our order to a fine figure of a serving girl. A minute later, the thoughtful girl brought me a stool for my feet, seeing that the chair was not well suited to me.

Most of the people were speaking quietly with one another, perhaps out of respect for the sleeping bard. With practiced efficiency the barkeep served up our order. The serving girl, whose hair was red as flame, brought us our mugs filled with two of the house brews. We always ordered from the house special selection in hopes of finding a hidden gem to add to our collection. She set down the generously filled mugs with a friendly smile. Then she giggled. She wrapped her finger around and tugged a lock of Kipp's blonde hair. As she walked away she winked a lovely green eye at him. He was taken by surprise and it caused him to blush in embarrassment.

"What was it again we ordered?" I asked Kipp who stared after the waitress. He seemed too preoccupied to answer, so I took a deep draw from my big mug. Usually I would sip the first taste of a new beer, but the powerful thirst and my obsession for it had gotten the better of me. Savoring the pleasure of the brew, I closed my eyes for a moment allowing the dust and rigors of the road to fade.

Kipp, still a bit flustered, finally answered. "Um… You ordered the house special Drinkity Drunken Dwarven Draft and mine was something called Dwarven Bread with a Head. The names are, let us say 'colorful,' at least."

"They seem to have a theme here," I said.

"What theme do they have? Giving their beers god-awful names?" I asked.

"What is Dwarven Bread, anyway?" Kipp asked.

"Dwarven Bread is a nickname of a variety of bread. It is baked with durability, not softness, in mind. It is often so hard that one can chip off small pieces and suck on them for nourishment; it's made to last a long time. It was featured in a popular story, and now it has caught on as a survival ration for miners and travelers."

"I wish I had asked before I ordered," Kipp said.

I poked at the odd beverage sitting in front of Kipp and said, "You are living dangerously, the reputation of Dwarven Bread being what it

9

is. I'm not sure how safe it would be in liquid form."

"I thought it just a clever name," Kipp said. "I didn't know it was an actual attempt at creating a drinkable version of the stuff."

"In retrospect," I said. "I think the only time the story speaks of Dwarven Bread in liquid form was when it was used to stem the flow of lava during a volcanic eruption, so I'm not certain if it can even exist at room temperature."

We both shared a laugh. Then, ignoring the possible consequences, I watched as Kipp put the mug to his lips, and tilted the tankard fully. Nothing seemed to happen. He pulled it away and looked again at the foam; it had only shifted slightly. He set the mug back on the table and the surface of the foam began slowly to level off.

Kipp's eyebrows rose, and he said, "Seems that it has an extremely firm body… for a beer. I'm just not sure how to drink it. Shall I ask for a spoon? Perhaps a chisel?"

I nodded and chuckled at the ridiculous sight of him contemplating the strange brew.

Resolved not to give up, Kipp picked up the tankard again, tilted it, and shook it enthusiastically. This time the foam head eventually slid off the beer, fell onto the table, and quietly fizzled. The "liquid" in the mug barely moved. After a bit more effort, there was a sucking noise and the entire quantity of "beer" slid out of the tankard and landed on the table. The strange brew kept the cylindrical shape of the vessel for a few seconds and then slowly began bulging and flattening. Kipp grabbed the brew off the table and worked it like putty for a minute. He rolled it between his hands and stuffed the substance back into the tankard. The beer slowly flattened and returned to its original shape.

I delighted too much at his plight and suddenly feeling impish, I drew a deep breath, and blew the frothy head off my beer towards him in jest. But the shape of the tankard directed it back toward me and the foam flew up and struck me full in the face. Both Kipp and I burst out in hearty laughter sharing the camaraderie of the moment. A few other patrons smiled to see what fun we were having.

Out of pity for the lad I signaled the waitress to bring him another beer. "I'll get the maid to bring you one of these Drunkity Dwarf drinks too. It's actually a fine brew everything a good beer should be."

Kipp nodded his thanks.

"It's time to do my job and take a real look at this beer." I pulled my notebook and tall thin test glass from my sack and poured a measure of the beer in to it. I held it up to the light and noted, "Nice deep dark brown color, slight cloudiness, lots of bubbles, good head, not too sweet, very nice indeed."

Conservator's Note: As most of you probably know, Del invented the modern rating scale for beer that we still use today. In one of Del's many notebooks, we found reference to this beer and have inserted it here.

Drinkity Drunken Dwarven Draft:

Look: 3.5 | Smell: 4 | Taste: 3.5 | Feel: 4.25 | Overall: 3.75

Served in: From keg into a pewter pint.

Look: Pours out a rich deep brown. Two fingers of frothy beige head that sticks around for quite a while, very nice lacing.

Smell: Pretty nice, better than expected for a publican brew. Fairly sweet, led by toffee and vanilla but also touches of dark roast coffee, rich chocolate, and toasted brown wheat.

Taste: Quite similar to the nose, black coffee and treacle lead the way; with a stronger feel of biscuit and nutty malts. Something of an old ale twang mixes it up with a hint of astringency from the char flavor. As it breathes the toasted brown bread, flavor becomes stronger and the coffee pulls all the way through the finish, rather than making way for nuttier flavors.

Mouth-feel: Much lighter than expected, and in a welcome way. Medium body, medium carbonation, light feel for the type. Above average drinkability, I could have a few.

Overall: Quite nice, and I wasn't really expecting much. A very nice balance between rich flavor and quaffabilty. I also get the impression that this may be a blended beer with some portion of old ale—Irish perhaps, which lightens it a bit and adds a bit of flair.

I passed the sample to Kipp, "What do you think?"

He took the sample glass and after smelling it, he drank it down.

Smiling, he agreed. "You need to write it up. Like you say, dark full-bodied flavor, everything it should be, even a bit earthy flavored. It should at least get an honorable mention in the guide." Kipp smacked his lips in appreciation.

A large man who had approached without our notice, voiced his objection. "We haven't been adding earth to our drinks for ages, and as proprietor of this inn I'll ask you to not restart any of those rumors." Then seeing the other tankard of Liquid Bread on our table he suddenly recanted. He shot a glance at the barmaid who was giggling.

"Oh my! That is from the old menus which were supposed to be destroyed," he said loud enough for the maid to hear. "It appears the staff was having a bit of fun at your expense, my apologies, please allow me to pick up your tab."

"No apologies needed," I said. "I respect a man who experiments with beer. There have to be failures along the way, or we never make discoveries."

"You are very gracious, kind sir, and thank you. I am Cecil Totalmire, the owner of this establishment. I must admit, I never knew a little quicklime would do that to beer. I thought it would counter the acid taste I was getting. Let me make sure you have our best." He motioned for the maid to hurry and she quickly set the new drink in front of Kipp.

"We are experimenters in the art of brewing ourselves. You see my friend and I are connoisseurs of fine beers and ales. We were merely commenting on the rich flavor of this hearty brew. The Dwarfity Drink one not that other, Bread with a Head stuff of course." I tried to reassure the large man.

A big smile opened on the proprietor's face. "Oh I see!" He seemed to be getting excited now. "Why thank you. It's my own recipe. I based it on a brew I once had during my travels. Please enjoy the beer, it's what our inn is famous for... that and, of course, the song."

"Song?" I asked.

The big innkeeper asked in disbelief, "You haven't heard of our song either? Well you must come from a long way off!"

Before I could answer, the man began to call out. "Ankle. Ankle, wake up! Anklesneeze! We have a request for our song!"

The old gray bard pulled his head up off the nearby table and fumbled with his ancient lute. He belched loudly then cleared his throat as he looked around grinning to be certain everyone had heard.

Next, he turned his chair without standing, scooting its spindly legs in a circle. The chair made a loud scraping noise as it moved across the stone and the legs bent at impossible angles, finally coming to rest so that he could see us.

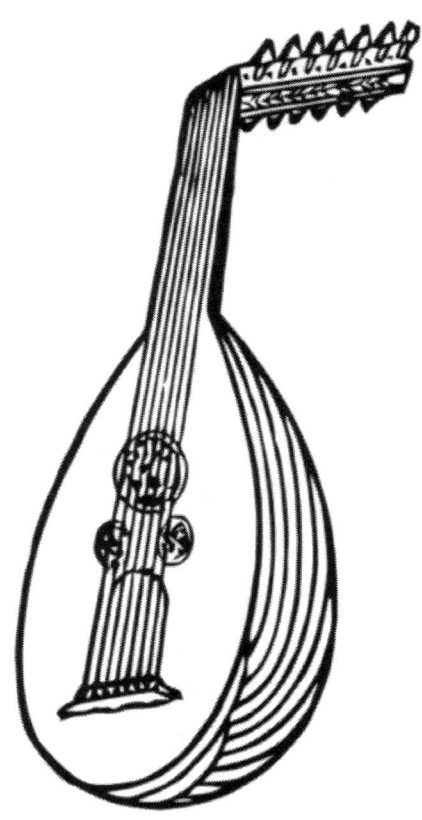

"You are in for a real treat!" he said. "I love this song! It's so exciting to share it with new people," the innkeeper said smiling.

The bard started strumming a lilting repetitive melody, which began as always, with the chorus.

Drunkity Dwarven Drinking Song

(Chorus)
A drunk-ity dwarf
He drank a draft
Of drink-ity drink, he drank.
And ev-ery time
He'd drink a drop
Of drink-ity draft, he drunk.

{Verse 1}
Then came a man
A gray old bard
Who shared a song or two.
The songs he'd sing
Made sad the dwarf
So he drank his mood anew.

(Go to Chorus)

{Verse 2}
The time then came
The king ar-rived
And called his men to war,
But drink-ity dwarf
He dodged the draft
So he could drink some more.

(Go to Chorus)

{Verse 3}
He drunk a draft,
A flagon of ale,
A pint of run-ny mead,
A glass of Bock,
A cup of Stout,
An-oth-er pint he'd need.

(Go to Chorus)

{Verse 4}
But now he's old
His beard is gray
His end was near at last.
And as he looked
Back on his life
He wished an-oth-er glass.

(Go to Chorus then end)

After the song was finished, the proprietor stared at us in expectation of a response. "How did you like it?" he finally asked. A huge smile covered his face.

"Yes, a good song, I'm sure it will be stuck in my head for days," Kipp said, trying to be polite.

"Yes, people say it does that, and that was the short version, would you like to hear the long one?" The proprietor began to motion to the bard.

I cut him off. "No! I mean... no thank you, we have taken too much of your attention already. You have other guests and patrons to attend. I won't hear of you wasting another moment on us. I believe that man over there– I pointed at another man who was sitting across the room– had a complaint about your privy."

The heavyset proprietor turned his head and began walking in the direction of the pointed finger searching for the man described. "Oh yes, I'll get right on it," he said and wandered off in that direction.

Kipp and I slid over to the bard's table, hoping that if the man returned he might have difficulty finding us there.

"It really was a fair song, it's just that a little of it seems to stretch a very long way," I said to the bard.

The bard grimaced and said under his breath, "If you only knew the truth of it my good man. I sometimes curse the day it first came into my head."

Sensing a good story, I asked, "So did you write the Drunken Dwarfity song?"

The bard had noted my short stature when we walked to his table and his expression was one of concern. "I'll have you know I meant no disrespect to the little folk, such as yourself. I truly mean no offense, good sir."

16

"No offense taken, good bard. I am a short man yes, some even call me dwarf but be assured I am human. Dwarves are not a separate race of people, they are men who have inherited their short stature from their human parents. Tis a common misconception and I'll never fault an honest man's ignorance so long as he is respectful. Therefore, think no more of it, I would like to hear the story of your song, and how a public house came to be named for it."

"Fair enough, sit back and enjoy your drink and I shall share the story.

"It was some twenty years ago, I was playing with the melody and on a whim I put the verse together. Soon it became a local favorite hereabouts and I could hardly play an inn without every man there asking me to favor him a play of it.

"Then later this man, Mr. Totalmire, whom you just met, paid me for the name. He said he wanted to open an inn and thought that it would be nice if it could be like the place where the dwarf in the song spent his life drinking. Kind of a beer drinking 'theme park,' whatever that means. He offered me free room and board if I would perform the song each night. Well to a poor bard who missed meals often and seldom had the comfort of a fire by which to sleep it sounded very good—I been here ever since. Later he named his best house ale for it and even hired a dwarf, um short, man to pose as its brewer and work in his brew house. Now he's been experimenting with beer, giving them ridiculous names, and I have been singing that song ever since. I must've sung that cursed song every hour for the last five years!"

I gave the man a smile, patted him on the back, and slipped a few extra coins in his hat. Getting the attention of the barmaid, I motioned for another round, for us and for the bard. Then I looked at the man to be certain he didn't object.

Then he said, nodding appreciatively, "Oh the beer is fine, It's just the song that I've tired of."

The bard continued his story. "But it's a regular gig so I shouldn't complain; I'm too old to go traveling around seeking adventure and sleeping across bar stools. Hurt's my back just thinking about it."

One of the patrons yelled out, "Play us the other beer song you do!"

Anklesneeze began another song strumming on the lute.

Death of Flowers and of Grain.

Flower of hops and seed of barley malt,
Living kernels ordained to die.
Sprouting grains new life's promises exalt.
Of flowering wheat, heads of rye.
Instead, men gather and roast them,
Grains ground to grist, bathed in wort.
In the tun their essence mix,
Of ale or beer or stout or port.
Dying hops and dying barley,
Bubbling up in an ancient broth.
God has given this gift to lowly man,
A mirthful drink with soothing froth.
To buoy the souls of weary men.
Amber drink of glee and cheer,
Dead flowers and dead seeds bring life
To thirsty men glad for beer.
A thankless man should sit and ponder,
Who granted us this bountiful glass
To dying men with dying hopes,
A gift of mirth before they pass.

We sat listening for a few minutes, enjoying the music and the fresh draft the waitress had delivered. This time she whispered something into Kipp's ear and he turned as red as her hair. She walked away again, swinging her hips a bit more than usual.

"Looks like you have found an admirer, Kipp. What did she say?" I asked.

"A gentleman never reveals such things," he said, still blushing.

"Did you offer to show her your drawings? Perhaps she is interested in our beer research?" I said, not wanting to let a good chance to tease him pass.

The bard winked at us and said, "Did I overhear you say that you are researching great beers and ales in your travels?"

"We are composing a guide of all the great drafts in the known world. I am the author. I go by the name Del Breowan and Kipp here is my illustrator." I prompted Kipp to pull out his portfolio of recent sketches from the clerics of Mallowhedge.

The bard looked through them with polite interest. "Well then, since you have been so generous, I have a rare brew for you and a story." He pulled an empty bottle from his pack and handed it to me. Pictured on the front was a gallant mounted knight in full armor. Bottled beer was still a bit of a novelty and the earthenware bottles were often saved for the pictures fired into the clay.

"I wrote the story after I spoke with a man who came through here several months ago selling these expensive beers. He was trying to get Mr. Totalmire to add them to his menu. He, of course, refused since he felt it would clash with the ambiance he works so hard to capture in this run-down privy of an inn... would you like to hear it?"

"We would be most honored," Kipp said while I nodded.

The man began his verse; although not a song, he strummed his lute in accompaniment as he wove his words.

The Ballad of Pale Pallie Ale

Legends long lost extolled the mysterious brew,
Known only to pure knights just a few.
Its secret to share was most heinous of treason,
Dire cases of need were the brew's only reason.

By aid of this liquid holy knights did subsist,
Still rumors and legends of its power persist.
The Abbots of Malmere brewed the liquid so rare,
For centuries monks toiled to make ale that was fair.

Readied in secret in oak barrels they did stack,
In cold tombs of a cellar kegs aging in black.
In forests beyond the abbey covered by ferns,
To the Canterhead wildlands our story now turns.

Dark Canterhead is a place a goodly man loathes,
Monstrous creatures dwell amidst its gnarled sylvan groves.
Ten merchant men blundered into the cursed place,
Enraged by their trespass a vile worm gave them chase.

As happens in legends, though all chance it defy,
At that very moment a strong knight happened by.
Dazzled by his gleaming that foul spawn with him fought,
Whilst the pureness of blade through scaled hide entry sought.

The knight's armor it blinded with a sunlit flash.
Mortally struck the dark serpent deep with a gash.
The gold knight split open the beast's scaly venter,
Its life force gushed out of its vile putrid center.

Disemboweled and beheaded it writhed in its gore,
Its spirit poured out until it breathed never more.
The knight's eyes now turned to the men who lay dying,
Found amongst the corpses a lone man still vying.

The unfortunate man's wounds so grievous he'd groan,
Over the man, the knight a prayer did intone.
A golden flask, the knight unsealed and unfastened,
He poured the brew sacred, onto his face ashen.

20

At once the poor man, old Killigan, was revived,
That brew was as fair and pure as he'd e'er imbibed.
He jumped up from the ground upon which he'd just laid,
No pain did he feel though his raw flesh it was flayed.

Killigan's face at once glowed suffused with a smile,
He thanked the knight for killing the creature so vile.
Seeing that still the man's wounds dreadfully severe,
The knight took him to the good Abbots of Malmere.

Weeks they passed slowly as the little man mended,
Sipping holy brew given by monks who attended.
Killigan a brewer of mead, beer and of ale,
This master obsessed about this liquid so pale.

When at last he'd recovered, the little man asked,
Of the brew and its wonders in which he had basked.
The monks would not answer him for fear of their vow.
To give him this secret they would never allow.

In darkness each night, the brewer crept all about,
In the hallways and cellars for clues, he would scout.
His search was rewarded a note tattered and stained,
A recipe it seemed though it hadn't been named.

Its ingredients and method he made copy,
A charcoal he used despite smudgy all sloppy.
The final day arrived when he left the good monks.
A copy of the secret he'd hid in his trunks.

He journeyed back home and his brewery long missed,
He gathered the grains for the unusual grist.
Pained he was lacking holy water to imbue,
So he boiled the devil from a measure or two.

The script next called for fine hops chosen by prayer,
So while roasting the grains he tried hard not to swear.
The barley it needed was refined and quite rare,
But instead just used whatever grain he could spare.

It called next for a thing the monks had called manna,
So he substituted a bean known as Guarana.
Implementing the long process kept him toiling,
He finished the brew by heating without boiling.

21

At last, it was done, and he tasted a sample,
Satisfied he'd made it in quantities ample.
The brew's impact it struck him he stood straight and tall,
Its energy suffused him, a potent cure-all.

Anxious to share it with taverns and inns nearby,
He brought them in samples for their patrons to try.
First, they'd puzzled its missing intoxication,
Each drunk it sobered to a state of elation.

Twas sweet and invigorating this it was true,
But lacked fun like bar patrons were apt to imbue.
Demand for the lively potion never caught on,
This result made old Killigan sad and withdrawn.

Wretched Paladin's soberness couldn't be hidden,
Their holiness and virtue shone through unbidden.
People in taverns were not towards it inclined,
Its most suitable drinkers he had yet to find.

Some kept it on hand for old knights with a title,
For each 'designated coachman' it was vital.
A vast supply of it yet lingers in storage,
But Killigan still struggles to pay his mortgage

Yet the old brewer he still travels all about,
Touting the wonders of this most marvelous stout.

After he finished, he took a long draw on the mug that had waited patiently while he'd performed.

We both applauded the bard. "Very fine story indeed!"

The bard bowed his head slightly. "I wish the song had a better ending, but that's what I have of it," he said.

Then, struck by inspiration, I asked, "Where can we find this Killigan that you speak of in this song, is he a real person or just made up? I would like to learn more of his tale and this unusual beverage."

"He is real enough, and he said he was from near about Freyhurst town, though I don't know where that is exactly, I do know it is to the north if that helps. If you find him, tell him I'd like some more of his brew since it helps me stay awake in this wretched place."

The rest of that night until wee hours we shared stories and songs. Somehow, I managed to find my bed and slept until late morning when Kipp made his appearance, quiet about his whereabouts the previous night.

We spoke about the story of Killigan the night before and how it would be an interesting story for the *Gazette*. Thus, we decided to pursue the bard's story. We departed after noon on the road going north, anxious to find Freyhurst town and this man named Killigan.

We traveled north several days and camped along the way. The third night of our trip, we shared a fire with a traveling group of clerics. The clerics were kind enough also to share their keg, and we all had a fine time. During the evening, I gave them a few of the tales my search for great beers had gained me. The clerics were impressed and agreed my book was a worthy quest. They proceeded to tell us stories of the fine brews they had sampled during their travels and I carefully recorded the details in my notebook for possible future research trips.

After the keg was nearly drained I told them of our new quest for Pale Pallie Ale and recounted the bard's tale. The Clerics were more than interested. They knew of Freyhurst and gave us good directions to the town. They also mentioned that they themselves had a steady need for such a brew. It was for the students in their clerical school. While the students are in training, alcohol was forbidden by school rules, yet they still have a powerful thirst for beer. They would in fact buy as much as they could find of such a non-spirited brew if it was as the bard had said. I assured them I would tell Killigan of their need if we found him. I got the information about the location of the cleric's school.

We bid the goodly men farewell the next morning and made our way north toward the city of Freyhurst. It was a fair day, and we made good progress, stopping only a few times along the road to enjoy the hard cheese and bread we had brought along to sustain us. Arriving late at our destination late that evening, we found a bed for the night and fell fast asleep worn out from the trip.

The next morning I woke to a tumult of people in the streets. I had expected Freyhurst to be a quiet town of quiet folk but something was amiss. I dressed quickly and woke Kipp and we went out to discover the reason for all the noise. Stopping a man who was hurriedly trying to roll a big barrel down the potholed street I asked the cause of the commotion.

"They've finally come to get Killigan and we are hiding our stores of Pallie Ale in case they come into town," the little man said, almost out of breath.

"Who have come for him?" I asked.

"The Paladin knights of course! They arrived early this morning and his workers all fled to town to warn everyone. They said the Paladins are going to hang Killigan for stealing the recipe." He began looking over his shoulder anxious to get moving again.

I did manage to get directions to the brewery from the panicked man before he resumed his frantic mission. Kipp and I followed the road that led out of town to the north and toward Killigan's brewery.

After several minutes of walking, we saw the brewery in the wooded valley below. It was a large building surrounded by barrels and stacks of firewood seasoning in the sun. Smoke drifted from one of the many stovepipe chimneys that dotted its roof. Its walls were made of roughhewn stone and the large roof was of cedar shake.

As we walked down the long hill leading to the brewery, we saw four large chargers, which whinnied as we approached. There was no mistaking the identity of their owners. The horses were massive and wore the heavy armor of a Paladins mount. They hadn't been tied, but they obediently waited for their riders return.

Kipp gave me a worried look as we walked closer to the building. I could now see the front door or what was left of it, had recently been torn apart by a massive impact.

Suddenly I heard a battle cry and the sound of thundering hooves beating the earth behind us. Spinning around in surprise, I saw a fully armed knight bearing down on both of us. The man and horse were huge, nearly twenty feet from hoof to plume, his silvery plate mail glinted off the morning sun, and huge clods of earth and soil spewed from the mount's massive hooves as it galloped. The narrow slit of his visor showed no face. Stunned in terror as the massive horse and rider rode toward me. I must admit I was terrified by the impressive sight.

"Well met, goodly Knight," Kipp tried to shout, but it came out more like a squeak. He waved his empty hands in the air hoping he would see we were unarmed. I hoped that somehow we hadn't blundered and inadvertently breeched some unknown precept of the knights code. This was easy to do with Paladins since they had numerous rules and regulations, not all of which were evident or even related the normal rules that seemed to suit everyone else.

The knight continued to bear down on us and I found myself wondering if this was how my end would come about. Yet I could think of nothing to avoid my imminent fate. Outrunning the beast was out of the question. The vibration of the hooves on the ground shook me more than even my own nerves; I doubt I could even keep my balance if I tried to run. Thus, I could only stare in horror as the man's claymore that was leveled at neck height.

Kipp regained his voice for another try shouting much louder this time. "Well met Good Knight!"

The knight pulled his reigns at the last possible moment and somehow the huge warhorse was able to counter the momentum of the metal clad mass before crushing the two of us. The knight lifted his sword above our heads. Instinctively, I still ducked the blade. We stood in shock as a cloud of dust poured over us.

A voice resonated metallically from under the great helm. "Who goes there, state your business or be gone."

I managed to recover enough to respond. "I am Del Breowan, a noteworthy brewer... Um, inspector, and this is my associate Kipp Lambert. I am here on official business; I have come to inspect operations of this brewery and its claims of making its Paladin Pilsner Beer also known as Pale Pallie Ale. We were told its story by a bard named Anklesneeze at the Drunkity Dwarf tavern and have journeyed here to investigate the brewery's questionable claims."

The knight lifted the visor of his helm and looked at us with a penetrating gaze. Looking at him somehow made my slight exaggeration about being an inspector burn in my mind as if I had just perjured myself. I decided that Kipp and I should be cautious in our answering of his questions, lest he come to wonder what exactly a brewery inspector does and from where one derives such authority. Also, I quietly reminded Kipp to think through everything before he opened his mouth. The lad has ever-good intentions, but it would take some doing on my part to get us out of this mess. The Paladin, still looking at us as if to pierce us with his gaze instead of his blade, finally nodded acquiescence. Then in what I can only assume was his version of polite, he said, "I insist that you men join in a council trial being held by my Order. Your expertise may be of use to us in that we may derive the truth from the web of lies and deceit woven by this same Killigan."

I smiled back at the Paladin. Thoughts of what might be the penalty for exaggerating to a knight began to cloud my thinking. I wished I hadn't been so quick with my story.

"Would you and your friend be willing to testify?" the knight asked, rousing me from my introspection.

"If you mean recount the song the bard told us, surely we would. Or if you wish to make use of our expertise, then I shall avail you of that as well," I answered.

"Very good, follow me to the door please." The knight rode the few remaining yards to the doorway. Next, he deftly dismounted his horse and removed his helm attaching it to a hook on his mount. Then he added, "Allow me to introduce myself, my name is Sir Owen, the Generous Hero of Sendegale. I am at your service." He offered a bright smile and formal nod. I was surprised to see the man's gray hair and weathered face–he must have been near seventy, but moved like a man in his thirties.

Kipp and I bowed slightly, returning the formality. I whispered to Kipp, "Best that I do most of the talking here, lad, we could be in for some trouble. Paladins live by the code, in the abundance of words can sin be found. Less said on our part, the better."

We followed Sir Owen into the brewery. Picking our way through a smashed doorway, we walked into a large anteroom. From there we proceeded down some steps to the main brewery floor. There were huge vats and casks filled with brews in their various stages of preparation. A number of large and small boilers were also positioned haphazardly throughout the large room. Each one of them venting smoke up the stovepipes that passed through the roof above them. The strong odors of fermentation and roasted grains filled the room, it reminded me of home. This gave me a measure of comfort.

Arranged in the center of the room, were four kegs in a semi-circle around a center keg. Upon each of the four kegs sat four Paladin knights, and upon the fifth there was a red-faced man in a leather apron. I assumed this was Killigan. It appeared they had been questioning him for some time. No other brewery workers could be seen; no doubt, they had all left as soon as the Paladins arrived. I looked at Killigan who stared straight ahead, his face set in an expression of anger mixed with insult. A discussion between the Paladins stopped as Sir Owen approached the group.

Owen began formally. "May I introduce Del Breowan, the brewery inspector, and his hail-fellow, Kipp Lambert. Allow me to present Cyprian Lord Felix, the Hero of Elfal, he bares the eagle sigil emblazoned on shield and heart." Fortunately for me their shields were carefully leaning against each of the kegs upon which they sat. Thus, I was able to put names with each of the men. The knight with the eagle insignia tilted his head politely.

"Next we have Goodly Sir Theodore, the Zealous Beacon of Mondeca, of the Griffin. Next, I present to you, Sir Darius the Enlightened Paragon of Archisere, sigil of the Dragon. Then lastly, our leader, his Lordship Sir Raphael Xavier, the Learned Rock of Hathemere, of the Boar sigil." Then as an afterthought he motioned in the brewmaster's direction and said, "And of course, Killigan the Brewer, our defendant." Killigan gave us a questioning look.

I bowed deeply. "Such a distinguished assemblage, I am deeply honored."

Kipp also bowed, remaining quiet. I was grateful Kipp was wise enough not to upset the knights. I had used the brewery inspector ploy before to get access to brewers who were a bit too secretive about their process. I would pretend to be an inspector and Kipp would pull out his parchments and begin sketching. This made us look official and had gotten us into many places we had no business being. I generally did the talking, using my extensive knowledge of brewing techniques, asking questions and inspecting the quality of their gadgets and grains. Just because there was no such thing as a real brewery inspector was beside the point; everyone always assumed there must be brewery inspectors and now, one was standing here in front of them. So we had never been asked for any credentials. I hoped that this occasion would not be any different. However, I sensed Kipp was nervous; the Paladins might not be as amused with fictitious inspectors as a brewer might be. A fellow beer fancier would most likely admire my gusto and smack me on the back sharing the joke. Too late to change my story now, I decided, so better to push ahead without fear as this might be detected by the wise knights.

Sir Owen continued. "These inspectors heard tell of this brewery's outrageous claims of making a so-called Pallie Ale and came to inspect it." The knight almost choked as he was forced to use the overly familiar term Pallie and ale in the same moniker. "Therefore, I felt they might have testimony that may assist us in our quest for justice, Sir Raphael. They were present for a firsthand telling of the story by the bard, Anklesneeze and are willing to testify to it. Add to this their expertise in the field of brewing and I believe they would make excellent candidates to be called as witnesses."

"Very good, Sir Owen. I agree, they are in a position to give us a valuable perspective. Have you explained to them the trial by four tradition of the Holy Order of Paladins yet?"

"Not yet, my Lord," Sir Owen said, as he shook his head.

The knight went on to relate to us the legal tradition of the trial by four that the Paladins lived by. The explanation was a bit long-winded by normal standards, quoting this goodly saint and that holy book, but it boiled down to this: Four knights decide whether someone was guilty and if they were to hang him publicly or privately.

As I listened to the knight explain, I nodded fiercely when such was expected of me and even a few times when it wasn't. Kipp too, seemed to retain focus during the lecture as well, since execution was mentioned frequently he decided, as had I, that it was best to try to understand how not to have a trial by four be held for you.

After the explanation was finished, I smiled and gave an indication that I was ready for them to proceed.

"In reference to the claims of our new arrivals. Allow me to ask you, Killigan, did you in fact tell your story to this bard, Ankle Steve at the Drunkity Dwarf Inn, as asserted by these men?" Sir Raphael began.

"Don't be daft! I've told my story to a hundred bards," Killigan said. "That is how you sell beer; it's advertising. You can't get people to buy beer unless there's a good story. No one will buy a drop if you say it's brewed in a big vat with pretty good grains and decent hops, you have to be creative!"

To his credit, the knight tried to ignore the brewer's disrespectful tone and demeanor. "I'm certain I would not know how one goes about peddling beer, but in every tale there is a grain of truth, so let us hear this tale and pick our grains so we may decide the truth."

"You're going to do it anyway!" Killigan said. He crossed his arms over his chest.

"Very well then, let us speak with our good inspector," Sir Raphael said. He turned to look at me. "Please recount the story told you by the bard, um... Ankles McGee or whatever his name, please," Sir Raphael said, growing irritated.

"The name is Anklesneeze good sir," I said.

"Yes. Thank you, proceed," Sir Raphael said. He smiled, grateful for the help.

"I would be happy to," I said. "But I want to state up front that I cannot be responsible for any embellishments the bard may have made to the story." The knight agreed, so I then proceeded to tell the story as best I could recount, with several interruptions by Kipp as he filled in details or omissions. Killigan tried to inject a point or two, but each time the knights silenced him.

When I'd had finished, Killigan's reddened face had darkened to a shade of purple as he seethed in frustration. The Paladins seemed satisfied at the telling and nodded. They looked convinced that the bard's tale was evidence backing their side of the story.

"It appears from the tale told by the good inspector, that Master Killigan did repay the good deed done to him with an act of villainy," Sir Darius the Enlightened said. The other knights shook their heads in agreement.

Killigan stood up from his barrel so quickly it tipped over. "I know that's the story that I told Anklesneeze but I didn't take nothing from those monks, I'm telling you the truth!" Killigan said. "I made that part up to make a good story. I guessed at the recipe."

Yet, try as he may, it looked that the matter was all but decided against him. It seemed all that was left was for the knights to decide the punishment.

"Hmm…" one of the knights mused aloud, "Public or private…"

Kipp whispered into my ear. "Looks as if Pallie Pale Ale goes from a chapter to a footnote in our book. It's a shame we couldn't have gotten some of the real Pallie ale to taste."

That gave me an idea. "Real Pallie Ale… that's it!" I whispered to Kipp.

31

I boldly spoke up before the knights could proceed any further. "Excuse me gentlemen, I wish to make a point of order." They stopped talking and turned their full attention to me. It seemed my assumption was correct, a Paladin would never allow a point of order not to be considered. After all, without order, there was chaos and, of course, chaos is from the dark ones. No Paladin would ever want to be seen as being the slightest bit against order and thus on the side of darkness.

Seeing this advantage, I continued as lawyerly as I knew how. "My friend and I, as mentioned, are beer and brewing experts, that is why we followed the tale of this beer here to this place." I paused for effect. "However, I have a problem with how the bard portrayed this man's beer. Especially when it came to the alleged recipe theft and whether or not this brewer is adhering to the fine arts of the craft correctly or if he has also violated the *code of the brewers.*"

This fictitious *code of brewers* statement had gotten the knights attention–they always could appreciate additional violations to laws beyond their own, and they seemed eager to add new offenses for which penance or prosecution might be required.

At this Killigan jumped from his seat in a rage, trying to get at me in an effort to thrash me, for he perceived my statement as a grave insult. Being threatened by Paladins for stealing was one thing, but to be accused of poor brewing standards by a fellow beer man! That was far more than he could bear. The knight nearest him grabbed him and forcibly returned him to his seat.

"Really?" the lead knight said, drawing the word out to show his peaked interest. Then he added, "I would be interested in learning more about how this *code of brewers* might affect our understanding and thus aid our endeavor to render good and righteous judgment."

Killigan gave a loud disgruntled, "Harrumph!"

"Proceed," the knight said to me.

"First, I would like to ask, have any of the Paladin's here actually tasted Killigan's brew to verify it is the same as your Paladin beer?"

"Well, actually, no. No, we haven't." Sir Raphael answered.

"May I suggest that I do an official test? I presume one of you good knights might have a sample of the original Paladin ale. My companion and I are, as mentioned, professional beer tasters. If there is any truth to be found, I propose a taste test to see if there is any similarity between the two brews. If they were the same brew, it would prove that he has stolen your recipe and is trying to profit from it. You see as a brewer, our code is that we must rely on the senses God gave us to detect impurities, by using all of these I hope to discern truth. Thus far, I have only used my ears. I must employ my taste, my sight, and my smell before I can judge the matter to its fullest extent."

The Paladins couldn't argue with my logic, but one objected, "The command is laid upon us that our holy brew is only given in case to save another's life, it's not for taste testing."

I had actually anticipated this objection. "Yes, but if you find him guilty, it could mean his life, so a life does depend on our tasting your holy beer. I assure you, both Kipp and I are men of unquestionable repute and amongst the finest in our profession." I wondered if there were in fact any others in our profession, but decided not to put too fine a point on the fact.

One of the seated knights decided that he agreed with me and pulled a golden flask from his pouch. Handing it over to me, he said, "A *small* drink for each of you, but go sparing."

I carefully poured the liquid into a small testing glass that sat on a table nearby. Picking it up, I closely examined the color and hue of what I'd poured. I knew a good show would be important. Then I held the glass up to the light. Strangely, it shimmered of its own accord, casting out reflections from surfaces neither the liquid nor the glass possessed. I puzzled at this phenomenon for a moment somewhat mesmerized. Therefore, I tried to focus instead on the liquid itself, ignoring the way the light seemed to play and dance upon it. The ale was as clear as crystal, with the slightest hue of amber just barely perceptible when I held it to a white backdrop. I noticed too the odd way the carbonation formed on the walls of the glass and how they rose to establish a head—precisely one bubble in height. In addition to this, instead of random locations triggering the formation of the bubbles, they appeared in neat evenly spaced rings along the sides of the glass, each of them looking to be the same exact size as all the rest! This began to unnerve me a bit, having never experienced such a bizarre characteristic in a beverage of any kind before, but remembering my audience, I pushed myself to the next step of the evaluation.

I held the glass now to my nose and closed my eyes inhaling deeply, smelling the contents. I could detect no alcohol. Its bouquet was unlike any I had ever encountered before; it was reminiscent of spring air or the smell of freshly woven linen hanging in the breeze on a summer day, very refreshing. At last, I lifted the glass to my lips and poured half of the brew into my mouth counting to twenty, as was my custom to allow the flavor to spend time on my taste buds before I swallowed. I handed the glass to Kipp who waited until I was finished before he tried it.

Kipp later said that at that point my face seemed to glow for a moment.

I was enthralled at how the ale lightly caressed my palate, each taste sensor in my mouth ringing in perfect resonance to the flavor of the miraculous brew. I was stunned and speechless as the effect of the brew overloaded all of my finely attuned senses. The flavor was one of everything and nothing all at once. I searched my mind to find adjectives to express the experience and was at a loss for what seemed forever. Then I recovered enough for my literary talents to re-emerge. I settled on the term 'rapture-epiphany' to describe the flavor of the true Paladin ale. Neither word alone was sufficient, both words together even seemed to subtract from the experience, but I had reached the limit of what mere words could describe, I was faced with the impossibility of describing the sublime.

Kipp now sampled the remainder of the liquid and his face too depicted pure delight. Later he told me that pictures and methods of artistic technique imbued his thoughts, racing at a pace he had never experienced before, techniques of depiction and ratios of perspective all swilled together in his mind as he approached the edge of understanding his art in its perfect form. Also, the toothache he had silently endured for the last several weeks was gone. He felt better than he had in years. In retrospect, I had noticed this effect as well, for weeks thereafter, the pain of my sore joints disappeared for the first time in my life.

As the flavor of the real Pallie brew slowly faded, I then poured a sample of Killigan's beer. The knights and Killigan watched us quietly. Again, I meticulously examined the color and clarity; it was much darker and had the normal bit of cloudiness for ale. The head was smaller than average but not missing. I sipped a small amount holding it in my mouth again before swallowing. Then I drank the remaining beer followed with a healthy burp. Again, Kipp aped me and did the same.

Killigan's Pale Pallie Ale was quite good, a bit different from other beers I had tasted before. Like the Paladin's brew, it was without the vapors of alcohol spirit that I am used to, but that was the extent of the similarity. It had a pleasant light flavor and a certain zing that made me feel more energized, not like the miraculous impact of the Paladin's brew but more of the zing of a nice cup of strong coffee, except tenfold.

Without hesitation, I pronounced my findings to the waiting

group. "What can I say? The true Paladin brew was nothing short of miraculous, fantastic and life changing. While Killigan's alleged copy was a nice refreshing drink of good ale that gave me a jolt of energy, it was in no way equal to the real Pallie ale. It is by no means the same brew. In my opinion there could never be an equal to it, the true Pallie ale is miraculous."

The knights began nodding and murmuring quietly to each other.

"With that established, now I would like to ask about Killigan's acquisition and use of this allegedly stolen recipe and its ingredients, if I may?" I looked at the knights who seemed satisfied with the thorough method I used.

They nodded seeming to agree, so I went on. "Let me ask you, good knights, could you describe the steps needed, without revealing any secrets of course, of making holy water?"

Lord Felix spoke up. "I have helped the monks with this task a time or two. I can only describe it in scant detail, however. It begins with a quest to gather the virgin snows of an unclimbed mountain. This is the first part of the process, of course, and this usually involves riding some kind of large flying creature and you must..." He went on with several more seeming impossible tasks in the steps of its preparation and then finally finished with, "The final step is the fourteen day fast of a thousand prayers and then the adding of the tears of the saint. I believe that gives you at least serviceable holy water." He then cleared his throat looking around to see if any of the other knights had a helpful contribution to his explanation.

"How long is this entire process generally?" I asked.

"About three years for a quick batch, the holy of holies water takes a full seven. Any shorter than three and it goes off," Lord Felix replied.

Grinning, I continued. "And the other ingredients? Manna for instance?"

"Oh that can only come from the loaf of St. Drury. It is added a single crumb to each vat by the monks." Lord Felix responded.

"... the sacred hops and barley?"

"Those are grown only on the holy gravesites of the monks of Andrew the Pitiful." Lord Felix once again replied.

"Hmm..." I mused. "Now let's find out how Killigan managed to get those ingredients for his beer."

I turned to the brewer who seemed to have stopped fuming and frowning. I hoped that he might actually be catching on to my ploy. "Mr. Killigan, did you use any of those ingredients for your beer?"

"Well, mine is as good as theirs—better in fact—they are just being arrogant!" Killigan said, still a bit offended.

Frowning at him, I said sternly, "Please answer the question."

"Well you know I couldn't get any of those ingredients."

"So how did you get holy water?" I asked.

"Well, I took good, fresh, spring water, and I boiled the devil out of it. Then I filtered it through fifteen layers of fine linen cloth, fifteen! Then I added the rest of the ingredients," Killigan answered.

I turned to Sir Felix. "Sir, does that make holy water—in your opinion?"

"No, that's how we make water for tea," the knight answered.

Turning back to Killigan, I asked. "So, Mr. Killigan, is it a fact that your beer has none of the same ingredients as the real Pallie ale?"

"Well, no, not exactly the same, but it's still good beer!"

"That's not the point is it? Is your beer exactly like the Paladin ale you drank at the abbey or not?"

He paused, battling his inner stubbornness, and finally said, "No."

"This recipe, did you steal it and the paper it was on?" I asked.

"I'm not daft! I left the paper there. I copied it down on my arm and left their paper where it was. It had no title on it, I didn't know it was secret, it was just a list of ingredients."

Getting an idea, I asked, "What did you write with?"

"Um... I don't know, I guess I used a charcoal pencil that was laying there."

"So you used the monk's pencil to record the recipe?"

"Yeah, so what if I did?"

"Did you put the pencil back?"

"I don't remember... No, I took it with me. I needed it."

"Well, there we have it, your confession gentlemen; your instincts were dead on, although you had missed the actual crime, Mr. Killigan is a thief," I said. "By the standards and regulations brewers hold sacred, Killigan is not guilty of stealing the beer recipe, as you had first feared but used it as an inspiration for a beer creation of his own making.

"He did, however, steal the charcoal pencil, he used to copy the recipe, and he has been using the name of the Paladin order without permission." Then I turned to Kipp and asked, "What is the price of a charcoal writing stick in the market in town?"

"I usually buy a bag of ten for a half copper," Kipp answered.

"Very well then, Killigan owes twenty times restitution for the theft of the charcoal, which, according to my knowledge of petty theft common law standards, is the usual fine. Unless you sirs have another?" I asked.

The knights looked at each other, no doubt realizing the crime committed was indeed not as serious as they had first assumed. They were clearly not happy that Killigan had gotten a hold of the recipe in the first place. But they had to admit that he had not stolen it per se, thus it could not be counted as the plundering of a holy icon, which was the capital crime he had been accused of. They understood, too, that by common cultural standards the copying of the recipe would not be seen as any kind of sin or transgression–recipes are passed among the common folk liberally.

I had to admire the Paladins, despite their terrifying appearance and tremendous prowess with weapons and killing. They were neither bloodthirsty nor intolerant of other views and cultures. I don't really believe they bought my argument about the charcoal theft, but they seemed grateful for my attempt at appeasing their sense of justice. They had settled down considerably once they'd come to realize the man was merely weak and not necessarily wicked. None of them was seeking a capital offense to satisfy some blood lust, these men were far too devout for that type of thinking. I had figured out that they were mostly upset by the use of their order's name and reputation to be connected to a common beer.

After a few moments of private consultation, the knight's leader announced, "Well it seems you have solved our case for us, good inspector, obviously your appearance here was divinely guided in order for us to bring this man to perfect justice."

"We knew all along that some crime had been committed," Sir Raphael said. He then winked at me and finished. "And the deterrent effect of this trial and the stories spread as a result of this day, by the good people in this locality, will help bolster our reputation and further our honor and commitment to justice. I believe I speak for all here assembled in saying the scales of justice are once again balanced. Now there only remains our coming to an agreement on the matter of the use of our name in selling this beer. That cannot be allowed to continue in the manner heretofore practiced."

After several more minutes of discussion, I finally managed to convince the Paladins to allow the name on the beer kegs to be changed to "Inspiration" (in large print) then 'Pale Pallie Ale' in smaller letters. Kipp was able to sketch a new label design that both the Paladins and Killigan agreed to.

> *Conservator's Note: Here's how this beer rated in Del's notebook.*

Inspiration - Pale Pallie Ale

Look: 2.25 | Smell: 3.5 | Taste: 3.25 | Feel: 3.5 | Overall: 3.5

Appearance: Pours a full white fluffy two finger head but fizzes away quickly. It diminishes to a small single ring and leaves no lace on the sides of the vessel. The color is pale blonde with crystal transparency.

Aroma: Barley malts, rice, some slight roasted grain, a hint of mustiness, and a faint pinch of hop trailing behind. It's very pleasant to the nose.

Flavor: Decent, but watery, has all the beer flavors—musty roasted malts, barley, rice, and yes, even a sting of hop.

Feel: The feel tickles the mouth pleasurably, not with carbonation so much (although it's there), but with a stinging hop flavor and lightly burnt malts. It ends dry on the tongue, parching the palate.

Overall: For a non-alcoholic beer, it has a nice feel and would give you a pleasant taste without the spirits. Also, it has a small kick that enlivens the heart and brightens your mind. No beer effect at all.

As part of this agreement, I convinced Killigan to distribute 3 percent of all of his profits on this beer to the knight's charities. Thus, he gave the Paladins ten silver coins as a compensation for what he had sold up to that point. He began to object to this deal at first, then I reminded him of the other options of Paladin justice. I whispered into his ear, "Publicly or privately?"

Suddenly the ten silver coins seemed far less important with this renewed perspective. Of course, he added the copper for the charcoal he had stolen to be given to the monks. Then in an unusual show of gratitude and good character, Killigan threw in an additional ten coins for the monks. He explained it was for his room and board during his recovery. This made the Paladins very happy with their decision indeed. Perhaps they had won a greater battle here today than they had expected, one that went beyond justice and bolstered righteousness as well.

When they left, the Paladins seemed satisfied things had been set right, however they made no apologies for the smashed door. Yet Killigan wisely didn't bring it up, he was very glad to see them go.

Grateful to me for my help, he further agreed to allow the inclusion of his newly named 'Inspiration' beer to my guidebook, giving me a promise of ten kegs of the brew for any "research" projects I might require it for in the future.

I also told Killigan about the students at the clerical school who would be very interested in his non-alcoholic ale with its invigorating effects. Killigan got quite excited at this prospect, picked up one of Kipp's charcoal crayons and carefully wrote down the name and location of the clerical school.

I reached out, grabbed hold of Killigan's wrist, and said, "Watch what you do with that charcoal! We'll have none of your thieving ways here, Killigan!"

The man was surprised and almost swung his fist until he saw the grin on my face. So instead he slapped me on the back and said, "How about a beer my friend? I'd like your opinion on some of my experimental brews. You inspectors must get rather thirsty." He winked.

In the end, Kipp and I had a fine new entry in my gazette and a new friend. We left the next day. On the trip home, Kipp seemed anxious to stop back at the Drinkity Drunken Dwarf Inn for some reason, so I decided to drop off a case of the new brew to Anklesneeze the bard. I spent the night updating him on how it had all turned out. Upon hearing the tale, Ankle got excited and set about composing a new ending to his Tale of Pure Pallie Ale. Kipp spent no little part of the evening courting a handsome young red-haired maid and seemed a happier man. The bard, Killigan, and even the knights had all become valuable friends. They introduced us to many stories of even more fantastic beers and ales, which we have featured over the years in our gazette.

The End

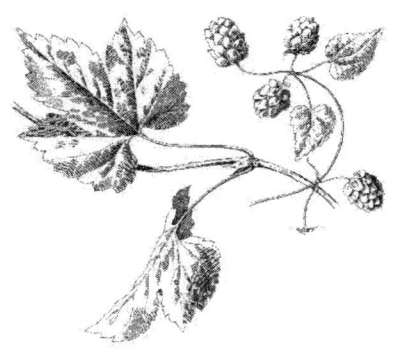

Del's Letter to Anklesneeze

Conservators note: This letter by Del Breowan was attached to the story and addressed to the bard. So we have included it for your information.

Dear Anklesneeze,

I hope this letter finds you well. This is a draft of our story. I'm certain after reading it, you can appreciate why I didn't publish it in the gazette. The Paladins are good men but they like their secrecy and would not take well to my revealing the details of this account. Besides, I have made an arrangement with them which I shall only speak of in person. Thank you for your contributions and continued interest in my work. I hope you have been enjoying the gazette each quarter. I must note that your last letter was both humorous and enlightening and I look forward to more of your stories and songs. Kipp and I will see you soon, for my hope is that our travels will take us back around to your home. As you requested, I shall be sending you further stories of our time together so that you may have them as keepsakes.

Yours Truly,

Del Breowan

ABOUT THE AUTHOR

Drayton Alan is an electronics field engineer who has worked with numerous new technologies. Up until now, he has mostly written technical manuals for custom products. In addition, he has developed and taught technical training classes for large organizations. He loves to teach about technology and other complex ideas by breaking down the core concepts into easy-to-understand metaphors and illustrations. Bringing speculative innovations to life in a story of fiction poses a challenge. To satisfy this challenge, he uses these same techniques for understanding and teaching existing technologies and then expands them to illuminate imagined ones. This latest book can best be described as "Beer Fiction" since it features beer and brewing as the focus of the story.

If you enjoyed this book, please read my series *"The Founders Gifts."* Available at Amazon.com and on my website draytonalan.com.

A young man finds an ancient device that changes life on his colony world and puts him at odds with a corrupt and powerful group of religious zealots.

What is Stout?

Stout is a dark beer made using roasted malt or roasted barley, hops, water and yeast. Stouts were traditionally the generic term for the strongest or stoutest porters, typically 7% or 8% alcohol by volume, produced by a brewery.

Have you tried a local Craft Beer from your hometown? Why not visit a local brewery tonight and sample a flight of different beers? Always be responsible with alcohol, and drink in moderation.

Made in the USA
Lexington, KY
05 May 2019